PEEK-A-BOO ZOO!

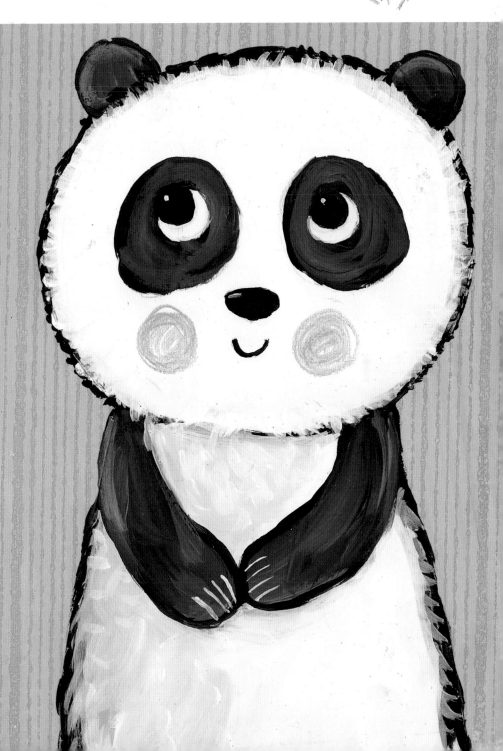

Peek-a-boo baby,
Peek-a-boo . . .

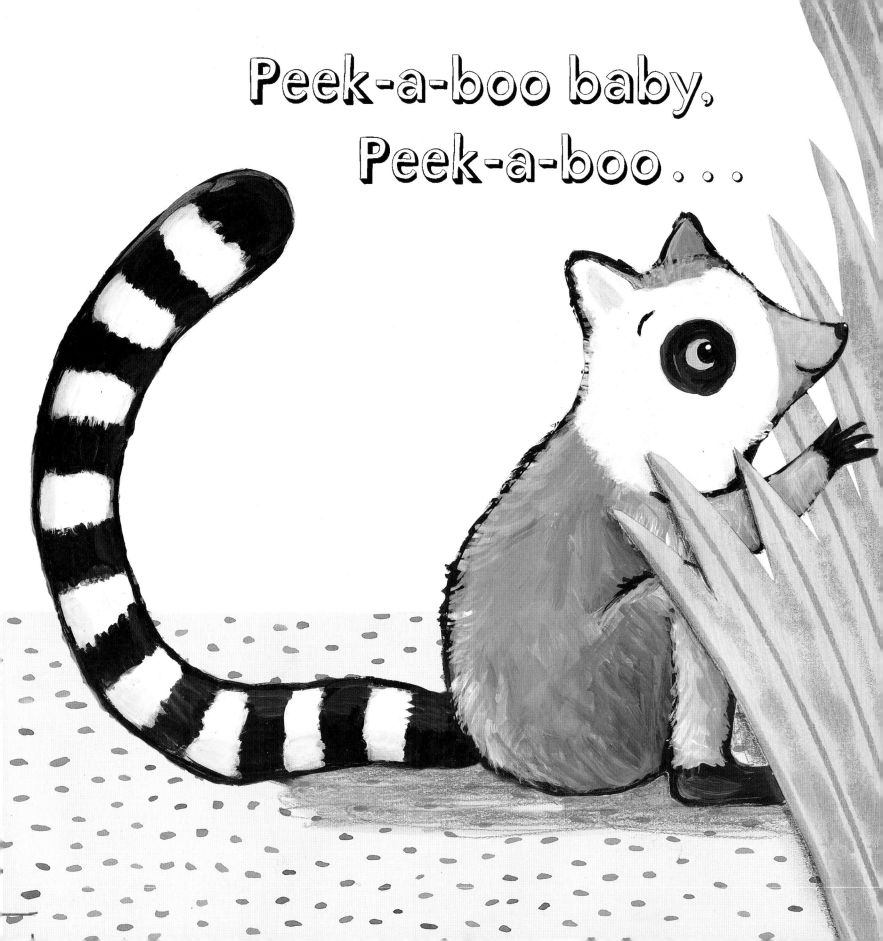

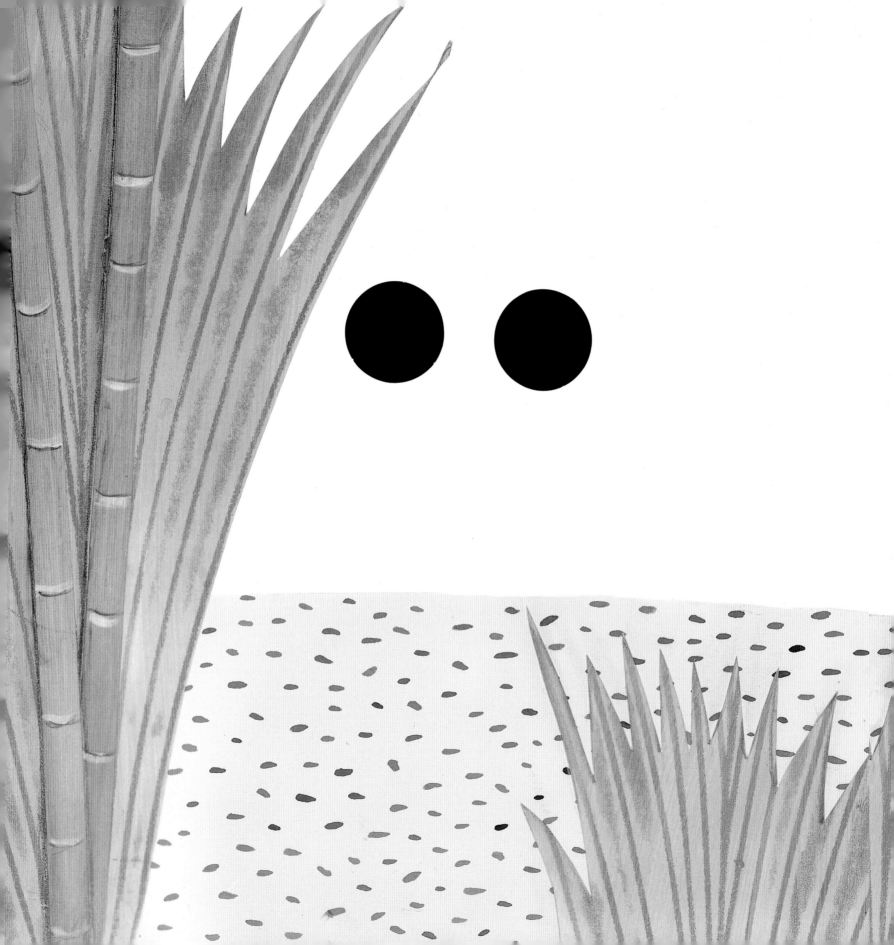

...two.

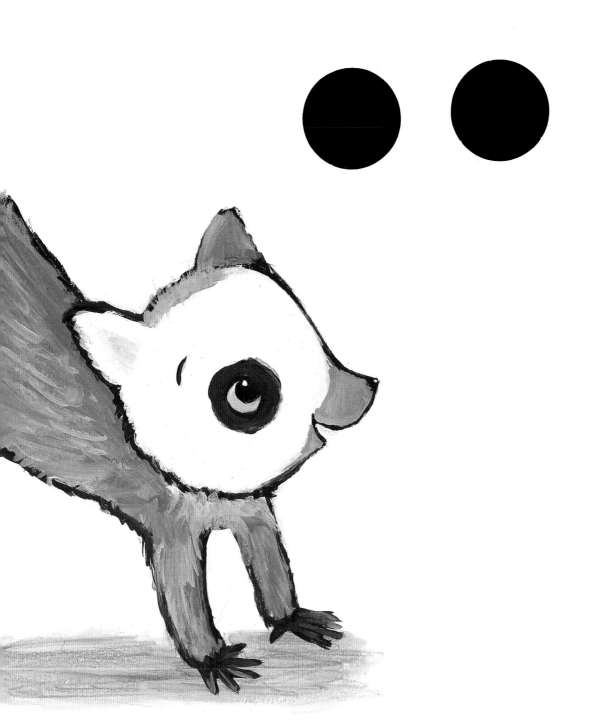

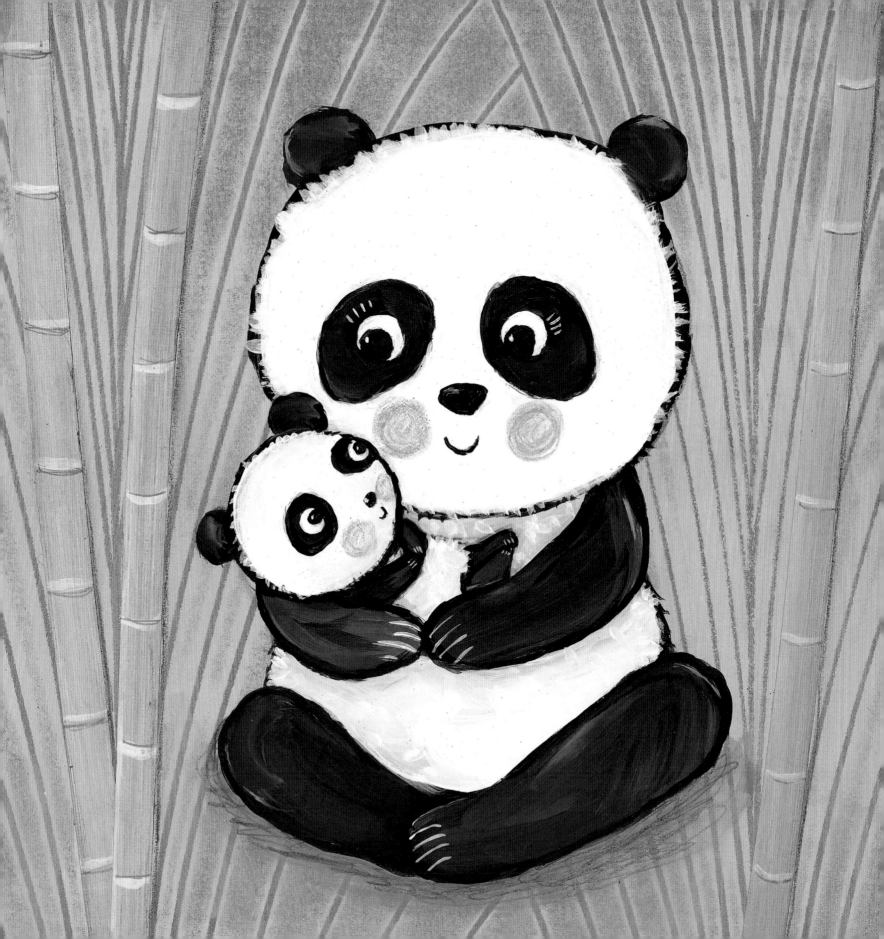

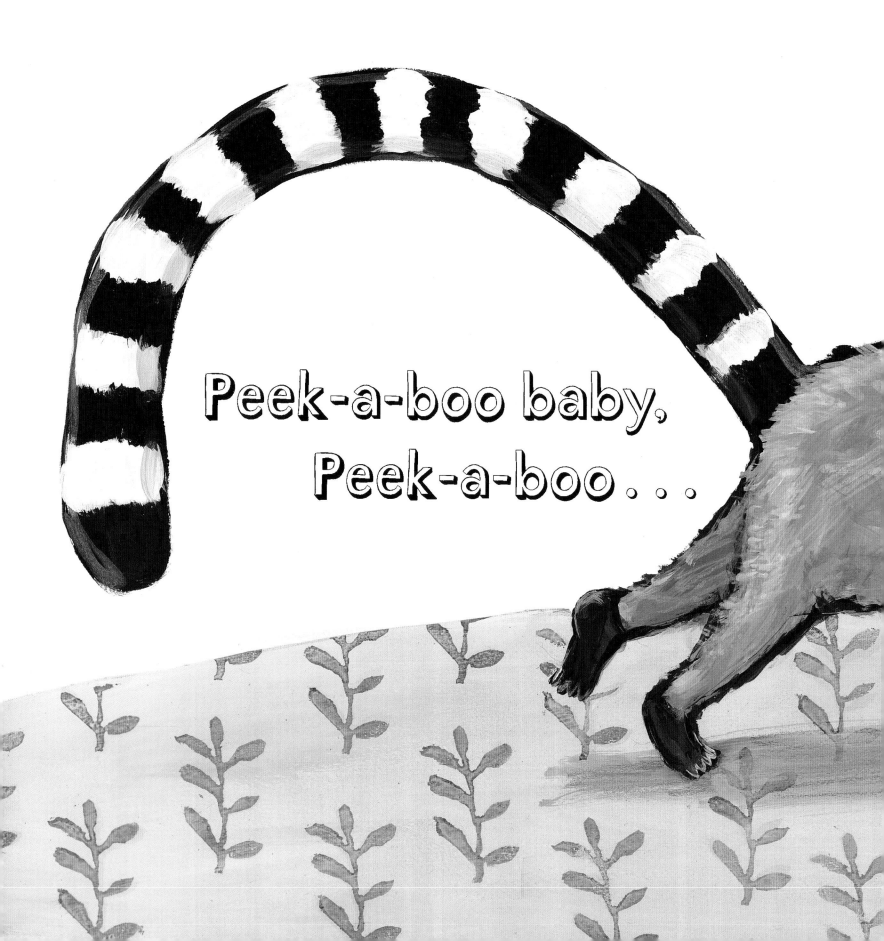

Peek-a-boo baby,
Peek-a-boo . . .

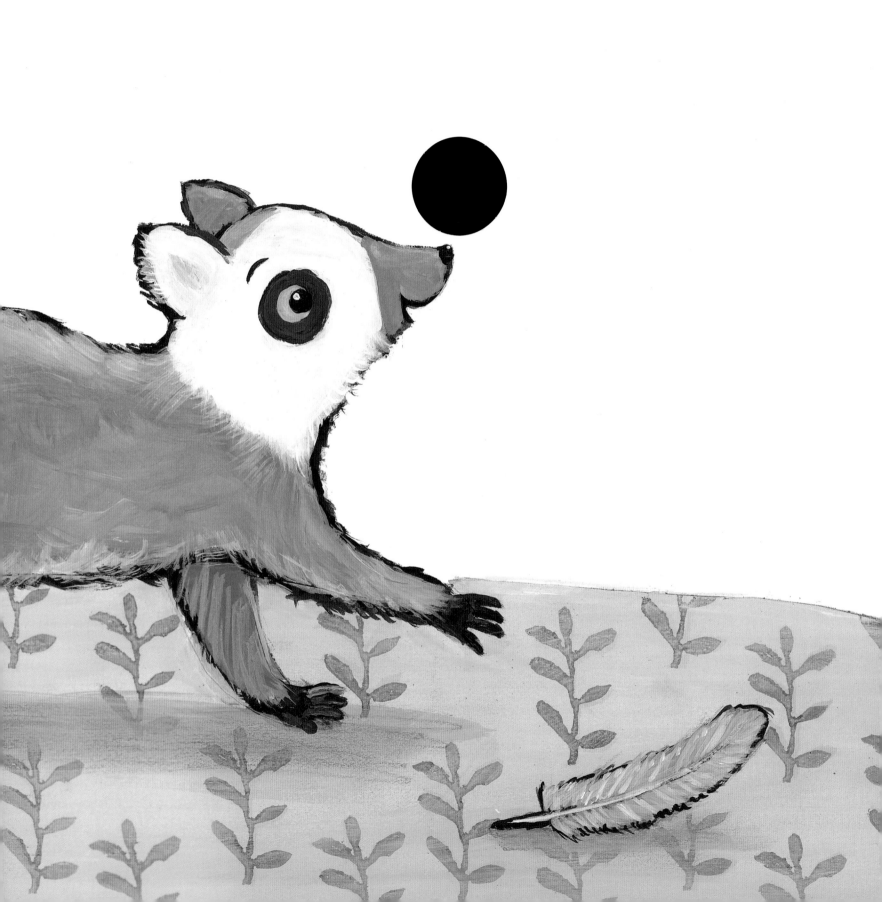

...blue.

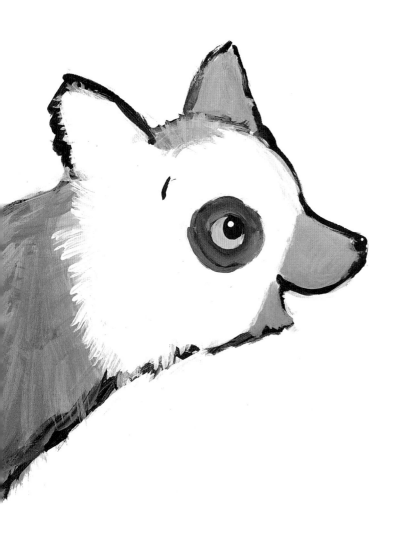

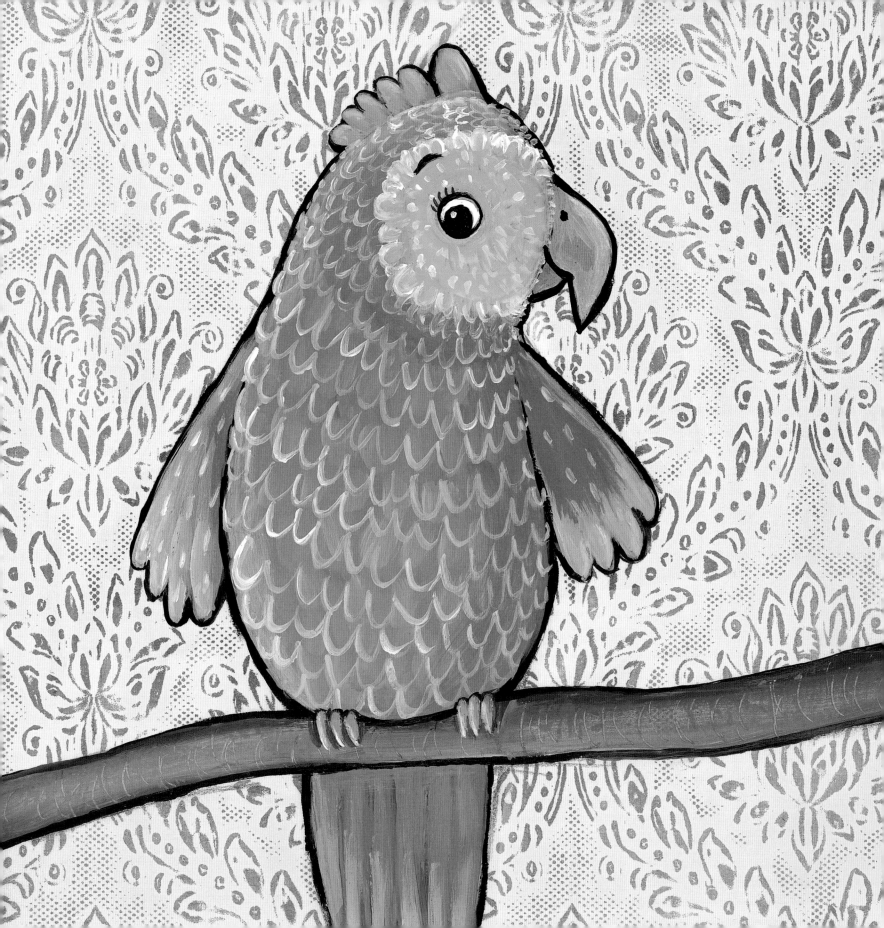

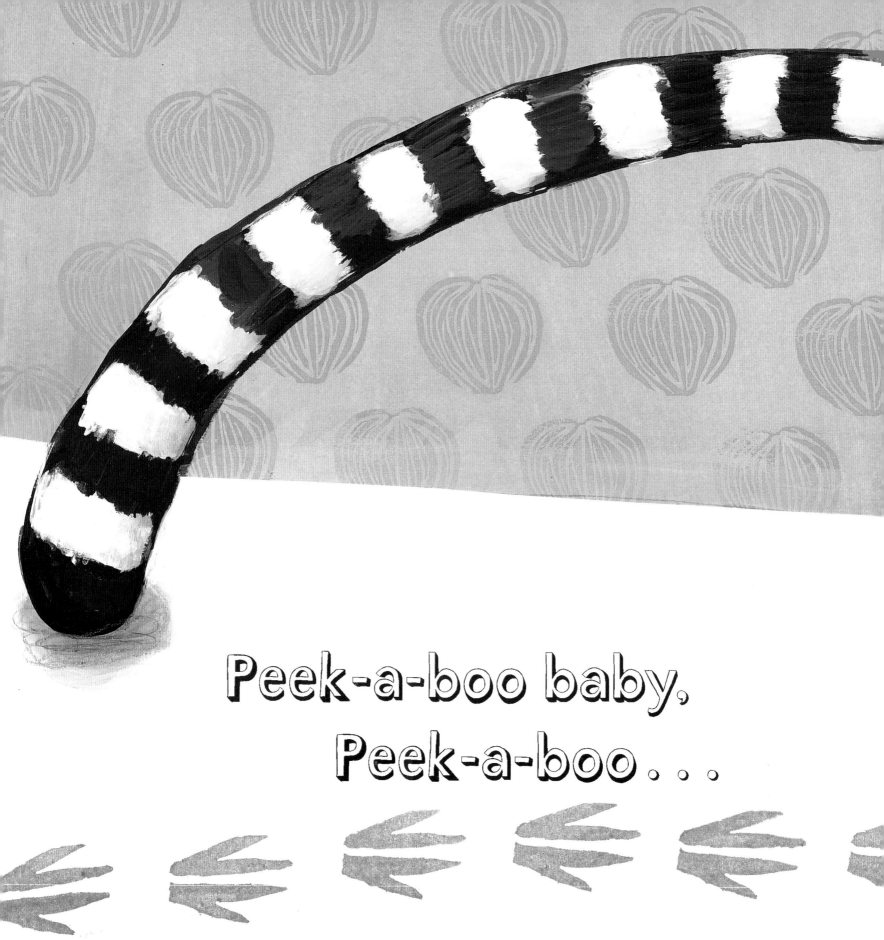

Peek-a-boo baby,
Peek-a-boo . . .

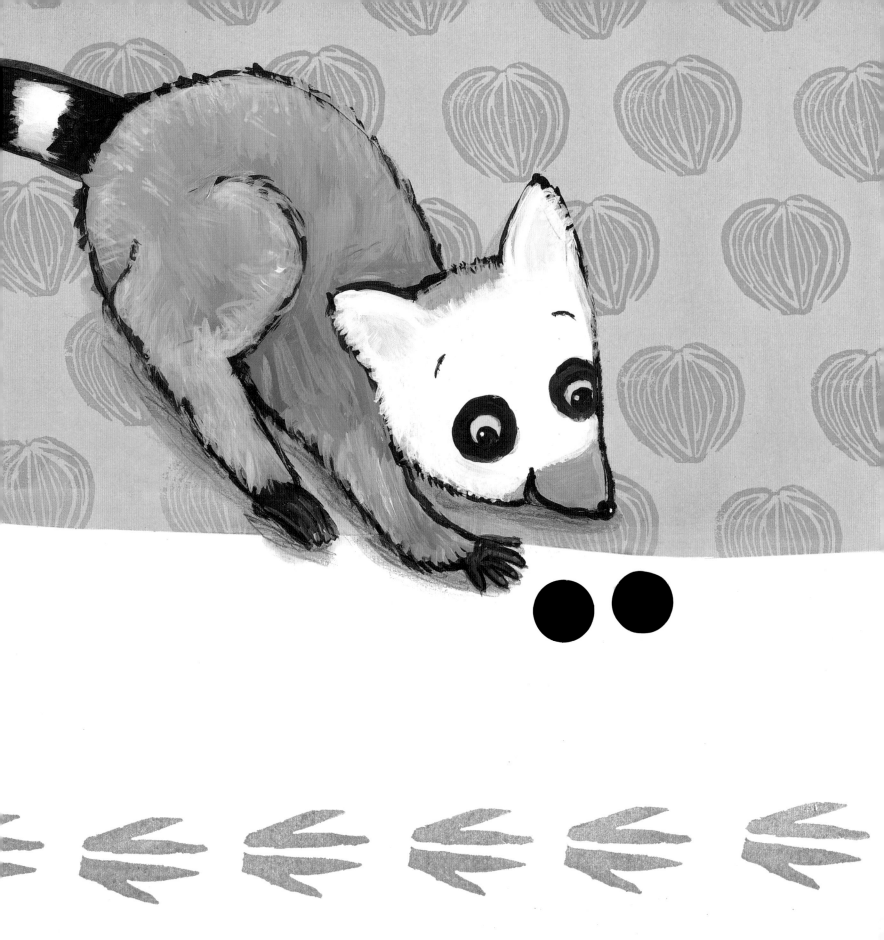

...roo.

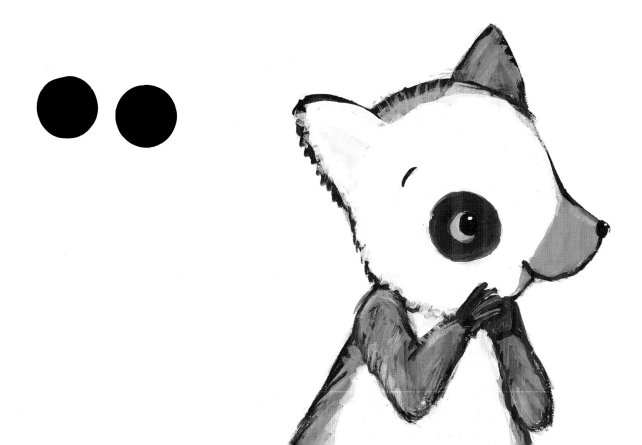

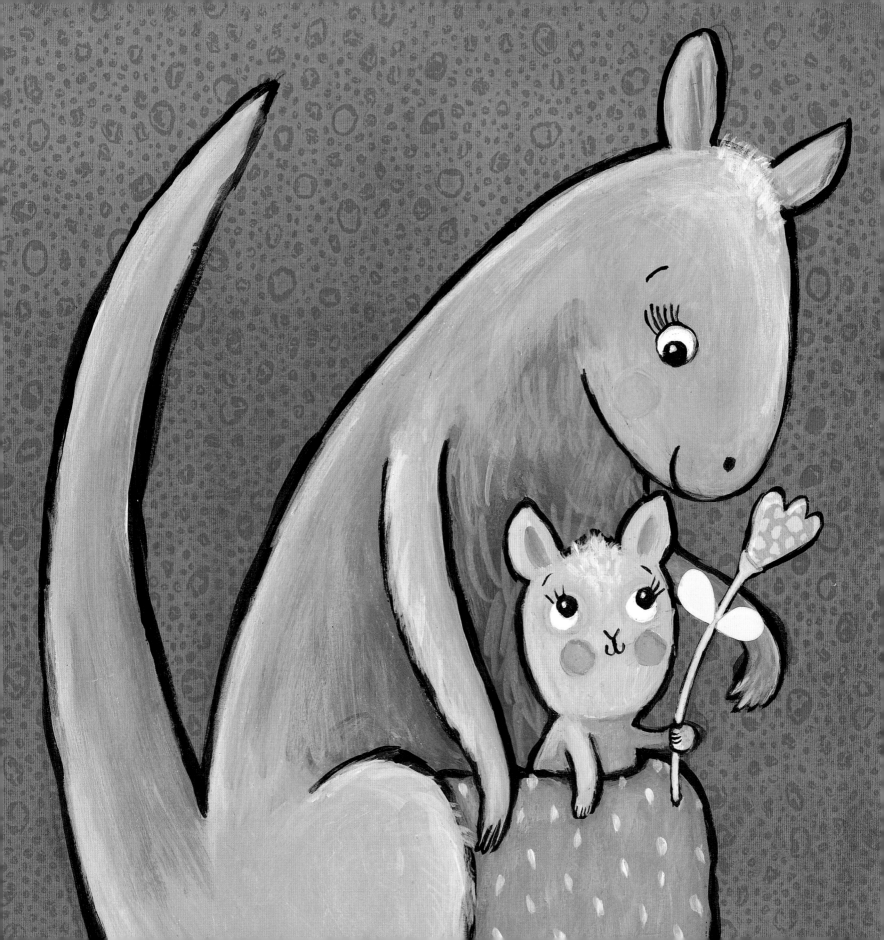

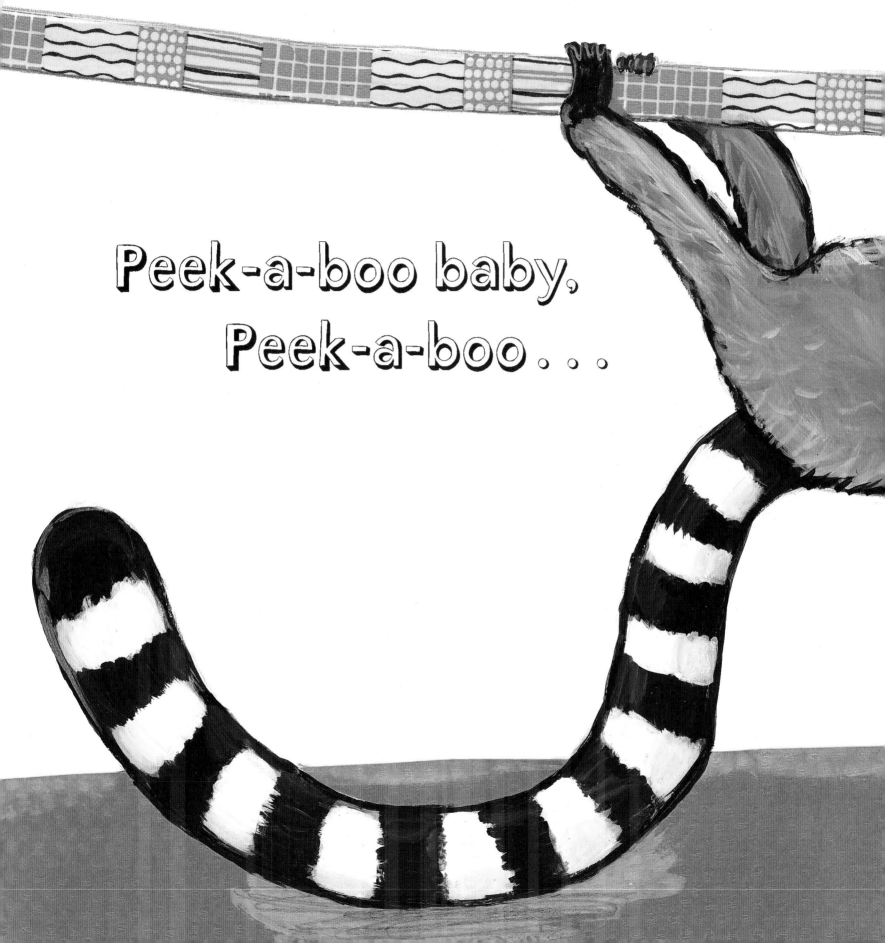

Peek-a-boo baby,
Peek-a-boo . . .

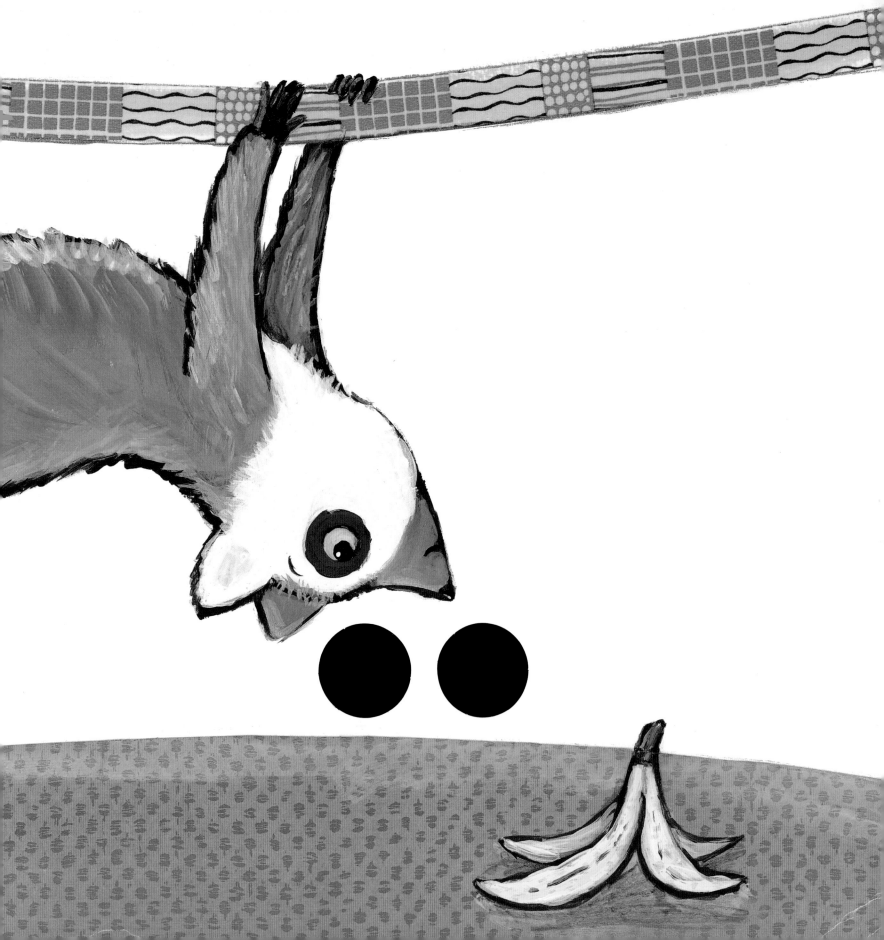

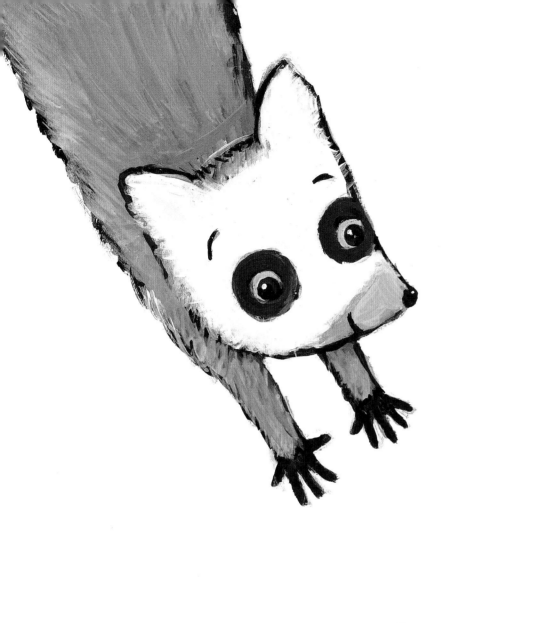

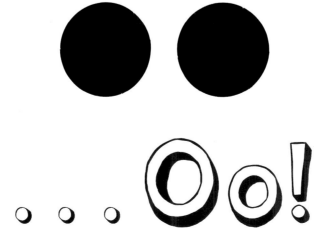

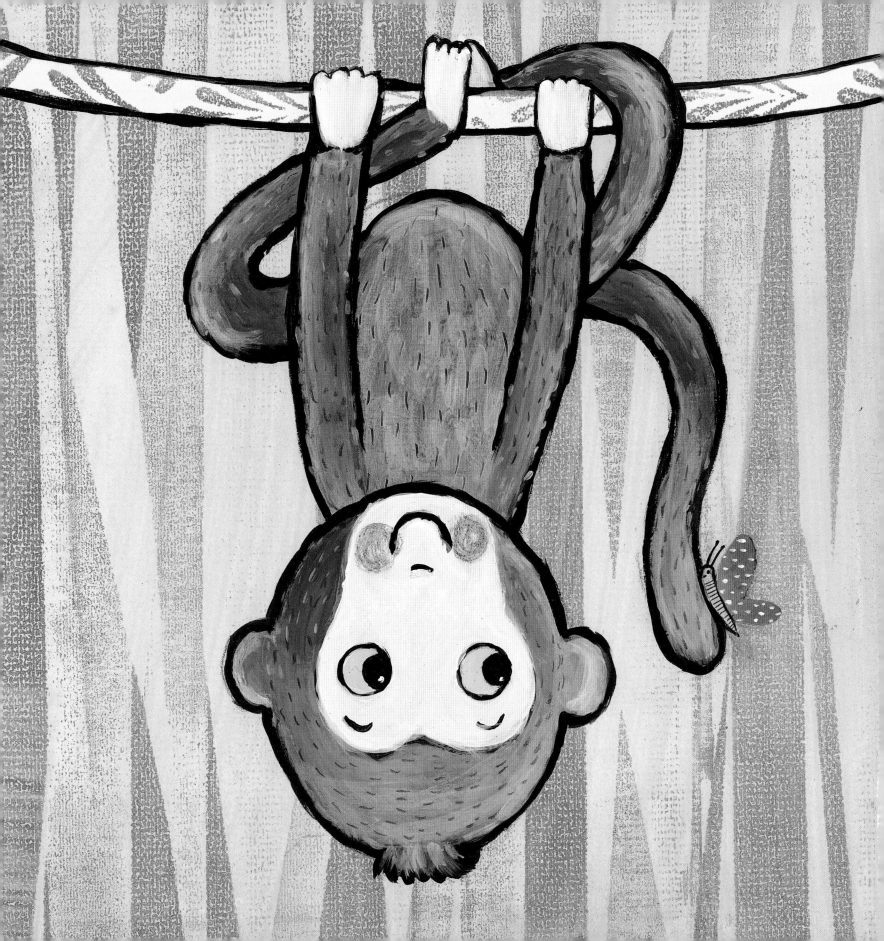

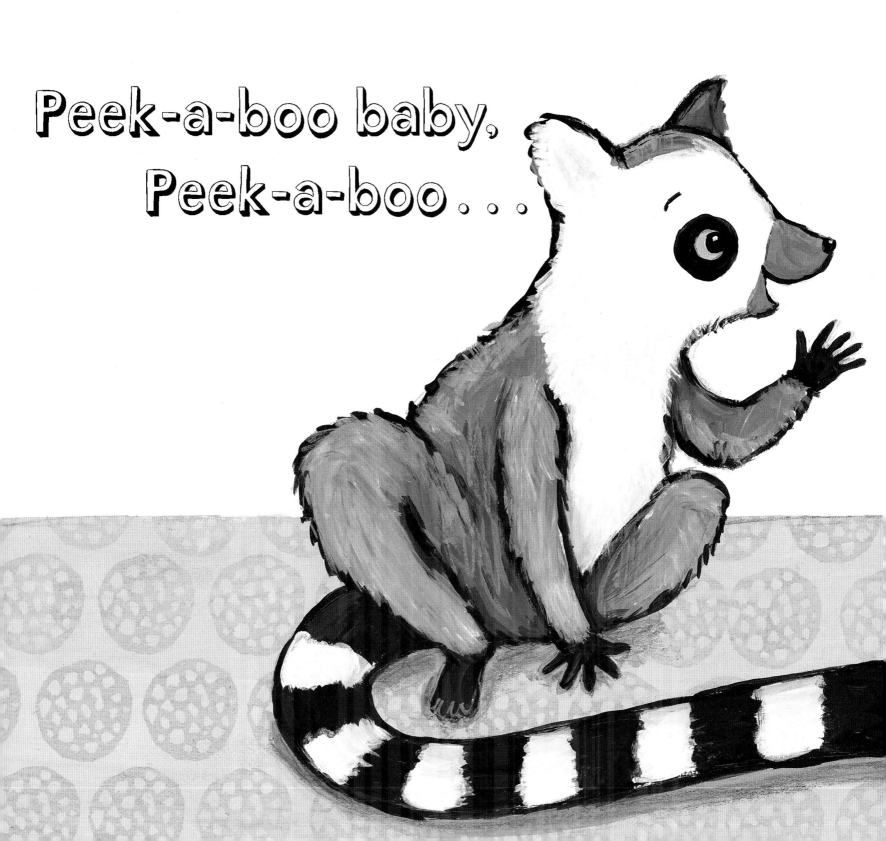

Peek-a-boo baby,
Peek-a-boo . . .

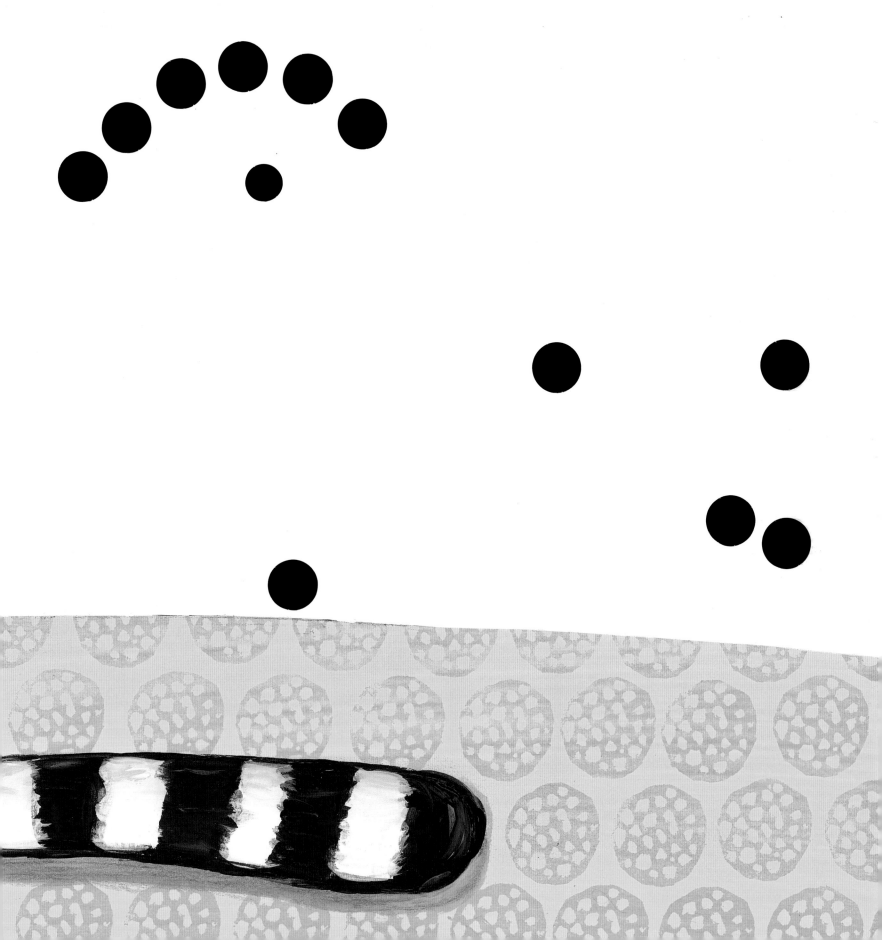

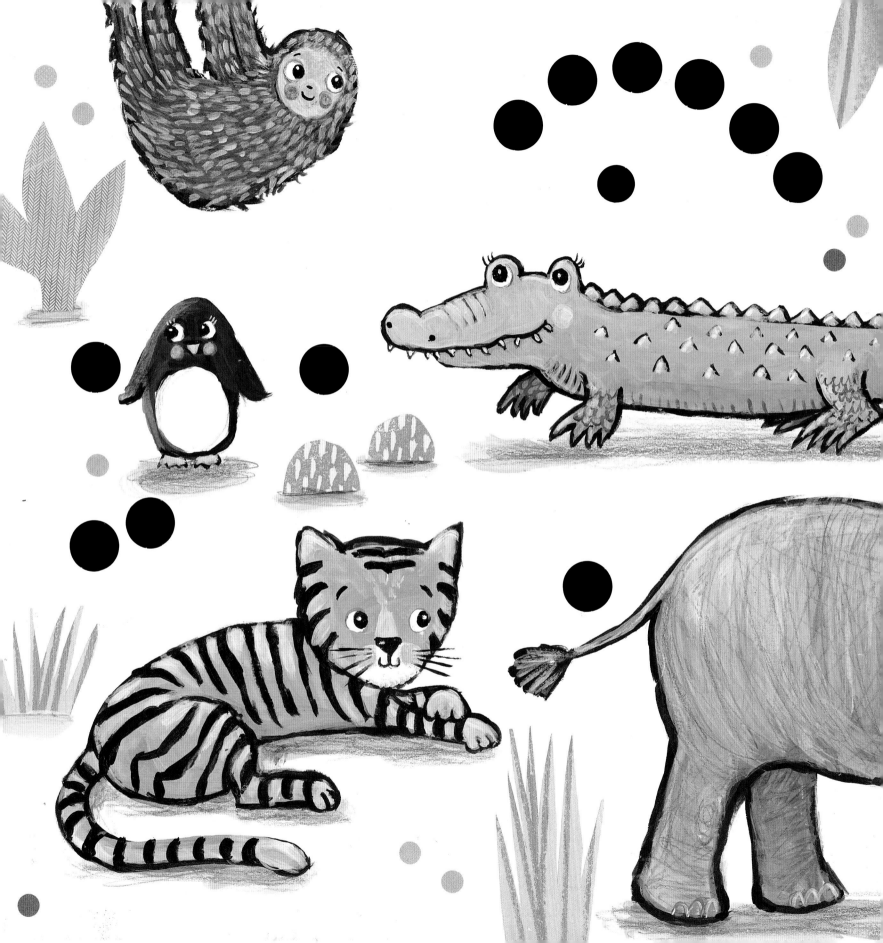